REMEMBERING
and Other Poems

ANTHOLOGIES

DILLY DILLY PICCALILLI:
Poems for the Very Young

O FRABJOUS DAY!
Poetry for Holidays and Special Occasions

POEMS OF CHRISTMAS

WHY AM I GROWN SO COLD?
Poems of the Unknowable

A LEARICAL LEXICON

I LIKE YOU, IF YOU LIKE ME
Poems of Friendship

(Margaret K. McElderry Books)

HOW PLEASANT TO KNOW MR. LEAR!

POEMS OF LEWIS CARROLL

THESE SMALL STONES

FOR ADULTS

THE CHILD AS POET
Myth or Reality?

REMEMBERING
and Other Poems

Myra Cohn Livingston

Margaret K. McElderry Books
NEW YORK

ACKNOWLEDGMENTS

"Reading: Fall," "Reading: Winter," "Reading: Spring" and "Reading: Summer" originally appeared as bookmarks for the Children's Book Council seasonal reading program, 1980. "Stars" originally appeared in Cricket, the magazine for children, September 1988. "Working with Mother" originally appeared in Poems for Mothers, Holiday House, 1988; copyright © by Myra Cohn Livingston, 1980 and 1988. "Osage Woman" originally appeared in Thanksgiving Poems, Holiday House; copyright © 1985 by Myra Cohn Livingston.

Margaret K. McElderry Books
Macmillan Publishing Company
866 Third Avenue
New York, NY 10022
Collier Macmillan Canada, Inc.

Printed in the United States of America

Designed by Barbara A. Fitzsimmons
First Edition
10   9   8   7   6   5   4   3   2   1

Library of Congress Cataloging-in-Publication Data
Livingston, Myra Cohn.
Remembering and other poems / Myra Cohn Livingston. — 1st ed.
p. cm.
Summary: A collection of poems about a variety of events and experiences.
1. Children's poetry, American. [1. American poetry.]
I. Title. II. Title: Remembering and other poems.
PS3562.I945P54 1989   811'.54—dc20   89-2654 CIP AC
ISBN 0-689-50489-6

For Jim Hoyl and Ann Neblett

CONTENTS

APPLE TREE

One branch is low enough to hold,
to bend,
to swing into the gold
of apples hanging on our tree.
Climbing higher,
I can see
across the empty lilacs
where
the poplars,
like green soldiers,
bare
of round fruit,
wish that they could be
wearing apples —
like our tree.

CHRISTMAS TREE

Covered in silver,
Sparkling in gold,
Hundreds of balls my arms enfold.

I am Greensleeves,
In from the cold.

COYOTES

You never see them
    cross the hill.
You never know they've come
    until
    they've sneaked across the road
    and found
    the garbage,
    spilled it on the ground
    and scavenged.
    Then they leave a mess.

You never hear them,
    not unless
    they've caught the scent of
    someone's cat,
    a lizard, snake
    or mountain rat
    hiding somewhere on the hill.

    And then they howl,
    And then they kill.

CRYSTAL'S WALTZ

(FOR CRYSTAL COPELAND)

When I dance
my small dance
of pink toe
and white lace

I am glitter
and spin,
I am sparkle
and twirl;

I am flower
on earth,
I am bird-wing
in air;

I'm the waltz
of white lace
on a pink
toe-shoe girl.

FIREWORKS

(FOR JIM HOYL)

The Fourth of July's
when I miss Jim.
That day I always think of him,

raising the flag high in the blue
of sky and waves at Malibu
and lowering it all wet with dew,

and after dark, how we'd all stand
around and help, the way he planned,
laying out fireworks on the sand;

pop bottle rockets we could fix
into their places on thin sticks,
and buzz bombs doing whirling tricks,

and pellets that began to shake
while turning into wriggling snakes;
the bang a Zebra cracker makes;

small cherry bombs exploding — loud,
and shooting Battle-in-the-Clouds;
and how we never were allowed

to wave the sparklers near our eyes;
big Roman candles shooting high
and fountains spilling from the sky

into the waves beyond the shore.
Jim had them all, and there were more
than I had ever seen before.

July the Fourth's
when I miss Jim.
Fireworks make me think of him.

FOG

Fog sneaks in,
spongy and wet.

In gray mist
a silhouette
of eucalyptus
shrouded,
still,
disappears
into
the
hill.

FRIENDSHIP

Sometimes it's only Betty and Sue
    who like each other,
    so that makes two.

Some days it's Sue and Ann and me
    who get together
    and that is three.

But most of the time it's really more.
    Sue, Betty, Ann and me
    make four!

GRAND CANYON EAST: FROM THE AIR

Red rocks,
layer after
layer, rise up from the
bottom of the Grand Canyon, like
walls of

old red
brick apartment
buildings; shattered windows
glinting in sunlight; faded paint
peeling.

IRENE

Remembering
el sol brillante,
the brilliant sun,

the hot ride,
el viaje caliente,
from Cuernavaca to Cuitlapa Gerrero,

su burro cansado y con sed,
her tired, thirsty burro,

Irene,
ten years in California,
steals lemons from the neighbor's tree

para limonada,
for lemonade.

JIM WHITEHEAD

Jim Whitehead came.
He was selling brooms.
He said they would help
To clean the rooms.

He said that our doormat
Looked a disgrace
And wouldn't a new one
Brighten the place?

He said that our screens
Were filled with dust
And showed us a special kind
Of a brush.

He said better things
Are hard to find
And whatever we bought
Would help the blind.

Mom looked in his eyes
And that settled that.
We have a new broom
And a new doormat.

KITCHEN TABLE

Our puppy
chewed
its legs all white.

Its top
is covered
every night
with homework,
dishes,
car key chains,
glasses,
papers,
Coke can stains.

It likes us
sitting round
for hours.

It's prettiest
when it holds
flowers.

LADYBUG

Ladybug,
ladybug,
fly to my hand!

I know,
ladybug,
you understand

I need some help
with a wish
today

and when it's made
you can
fly away!

LEAF BOATS

Rain
down
the
drain
        is a waterfall.

A leaf sails along.
A twig starts to float.

I watch
as they bob
and they bounce
down
the
drain.

I see
the rain
drowning
each tiny, wet boat.

LINCOLN

Lincoln
stares
from our classroom wall.

History says
he was lanky, tall.
History says
that he borrowed books
and some people laughed
at his rumpled looks.

Born in a cabin,
he would be
the President
who set slaves free.

He gave the Gettysburg Address.
Except for George Washington
Lincoln was best
of all the presidents,
and wise.

I can sort of see that
when I stare at his eyes.

LONG BEACH: FEBRUARY

Even the moon lies
on its back, rolling over
to stare into space.

MR. PETTENGILL

Mr. Pettengill
stands on the walk
waiting for someone
who wants to
talk
about the way
the weather will be
or what he saw
on late
TV
or where his
next-door neighbor went
or politics
or rising
rent
or anything
he wants to know,
so I just nod
and say
hello
and something or other
about the sun
and then I smile
and then I
run!

THE NECKLACE

I am the pirate
who sails the high seas.

Jewels are my treasures
and best of all these

is a necklace of gold
set with pearls, milky white,
worn by a mermaid
I captured one night

       who slithered away to her cave in the sand
       leaving this chain in the clutch of my hand;

a luminous necklace,
a chain sparkling bright,
the gift of a mermaid
I captured one night.

NIGHT LIGHT

Lamp is OFF
    is ON

    is light

    is friend
to me
against
the night.

NOVEMBER ACORN

Green face
wears
a
tassled
cap.

Along comes wind.

The tassel
snaps

so
cap
and
green face

tumble
down

and green face
turns
a
shiny
brown.

O SAY

". . . neither shall they learn war any more."

ISAIAH 2:4

MICAH 4:3

Can you see
the bursting bombs?
Soldiers
fall
to
unknown tombs?
tanks?
jet fighters?
smoking guns?
dead guerrillas?
bloody dunes?
crumbled buildings?
cities burned?

We never learned.
We never learned.

OWL OF NIGHT

Owl
is the one
who knows
nightfall,

knows
the dark,
the song
to call   out of the trees
across the gloom
asking questions
in my room.

I hear you,
owl of night,
I hear,
and all my answers hide
in fear.

PIANO RECITAL

We were invited to Mrs. Chaudet's
for a piano recital.
I had to play

a Mozart sonata. It wasn't much fun.
Boy, was I glad when
it was done.

There was a Bach piece Susan played.
Then we ate cupcakes
and drank lemonade.

Mrs. Chaudet said we all did well.
She *had* to say that,
but I heard someone tell

someone else that if Mozart and Bach
had heard us play
they'd have died of shock!

PIGEONS & POPCORN

At Union Station the pigeons flock,
swooping down from where the clock
tells people when their trains will go,
and this is how the pigeons know
that people wait. They look around
for something left there on the ground
that they can eat. One pigeon ate
a Frito on a paper plate.
But what they really like the most,
better than crusts of bread or toast,
is popcorn—popcorn, fluffy white.
You give them some, they almost bite
your fingers off, they like it so.
I bought a whole bag once. Below
my feet the pigeons stood
and let me know it would be good
if they could have a little treat.
I didn't really need to eat.
I threw a kernel, then threw two.
Down from the clock the pigeons flew
and soon I'd given it away.
There was no more. But pigeons stay
around you for a little bit
until they see where people sit
with popcorn bags, and then they beg
beneath another person's leg,
or if a train is going, flock
back to the tiles near the clock
and sit around and sort of coo
and wait, just like the people do.

POISON IVY

(FOR MARGARET)

We told her it grew
at the edge of the lot.

We said to be careful
but she forgot.

Now she's all itchy
and patchy and rough.

Her skin is in blisters
and covered with stuff;

We fixed baking soda
and washed her with soap

and calamine lotion,
but what a big dope

when we told her it grew
at the edge of the lot

and she went there to play
and simply forgot.

POSSIBILITY

"If you'd care to consider the matter,"
Said the egg in its shell, "you'd be fatter
    If you leave me alone;
    I will grow skin and bone
And taste better by far on a platter!"

PUZZLE

John left school.
It was sad.
There wasn't anything he had

we needed
or we even liked.
Had no skateboard. Had no bike.

He wore old shorts,
a frayed old sweater.
Guess he never had much better.

But John was cool,
a real nice guy.
Nobody knew when his mom came by

to pick him up.
He was moving away.
He never came to school next day.

He left his notebook. Left his pen.
He might come back
but who knows when?

What puzzles all of us
is why
he left, and never said good-bye.

RAIN: A HAIKU SEQUENCE

1.

One last blue patch of
sky about to be swallowed
by thundering clouds . . .

2.

What a strange carpet
the rain weaves with its pattern
of leaves and brown twigs . . .

3.

Another raindrop
and the stream will overflow
into the meadow . . .

4.

Searching for only
one clear puddle, I'll find my
rain-drenched reflection . . .

5.

When the rain has stopped,
mourning dove, you can begin
your singing again . . .

READCREST DRIVE

In our mountains
   yucca trees
   lift fuzzy heads
   to catch the breeze.

Eucalyptus shed their skin.

Palm trees dig their gray toes in
the ground. Their fronds
dance everywhere,

and Scotch broom
sweeps the autumn air.

READING: FALL

Base calling fall
Come in. You're clear.
I hear you
Whistling in my ear.
I sight
Your wind bend down
The trees.
I spot you
Scattering the leaves.
I feel you
Chase me back to school.
To books, to reading . . .
Base, you're cool
The way you read it
Every year.
Base calling fall . . .
Fall out.
Base clear.

READING: WINTER

O it's neat reading out in the snow!
It's the coziest place you can go.
  It's such fun when you freeze
  With a book on your knees
And it's Celsius twenty below!

Never mind when a winter storm blows!
Never care that you've frozen your toes!
  It's so shivery nice
  When a thin cake of ice
Glues the page to the end of your nose!

What if icicles drip from your chin?
What if snowdrifts and frost nip you in?
  If your fingers turn blue
  When a chapter is through
Think of all the warm places you've been!

READING: SPRING

Well,
if it isn't
baseball/skateboard/
jump rope/hopscotch
SPRING
I just don't know my
marbles/robin/blooming/SEASON
greening up the trees,
blueing up the sky,
yelling to come outside and play.

So,
I'll put you here,
bookmark, to save
the place where I
stopped
reading of a time
when once upon a spring, this kid
opened the window
and heard a lot of
yelling to come outside and play.

READING: SUMMER

Summer is with it,
   she's wild,
   she likes
   bare legs and cutoffs
   and camping
   and hikes;
   she dives in deep water,
   she wades in a stream,
   she guzzles cold drinks
   and she drowns in ice cream;
   she runs barefoot,
   she picnics,
   she fishes,
   digs bait,
   she pitches a tent
   and she stays up too late
   while she counts out the stars,
   swats mosquitoes and flies,
   hears crickets,
   smells pine trees,
   spies night-creature eyes;
   she rides bareback,
   goes sailing,
   plays tennis,
   climbs trees;
   she soaks in the sunshine;
   she gulps in a breeze;
   she tastes the warm air
   on the end of her tongue, .

and she falls asleep
reading
alone
in the sun.

REMEMBERING

The waves washed in a mountain of shells.
I stayed for hours, picking them through.
There were hundreds of olives, hundreds of snails,
a shining cowry,
and one or two
pieces of broken razor clams
mixed with some barnacles and cones.
I washed them off in a paper cup.
Dumping the sand,
I took them home
and poured them into a tall glass jar
where they mix in spirals of pink and brown.
Tiny black rocks are caught in the snails.
A lot have holes. The sand sifts down.

Sometimes I catch a smell of the sea
from the barnacles and the snails and cones.
They are all that is left of an August day
when the waves washed in
the ocean's bones.

SCHOOL PLAY

I played the princess.
I had to stay
inside a barrel.
The prince hid away
in a keg right beside me.
Our hearts nearly sank
when the Pirate King said
we would both walk the plank.
Then our captain appeared
and he offered them gold
as a ransom, and that's when
the Pirate King told
us to come out
and plead our case,
and I climbed out and
slipped
and fell flat
on my face.

But it wasn't so bad
in the ending
because
all the audience gave us
a lot of
applause.

SECRET

The secret I told you
I shouldn't have told,
but you're my best friend and
it's too hard to hold
a secret inside me.

I tried,
but I knew
it could still be a secret —

if I told you.

SKY TALES OF THE ASSINIBOIN INDIANS

I

The sky is a blue vault
a great blue arch
resting on the plain

so far away
we cannot see
where it begins.

Flies,
spiders,
birds
hang on to the sky
with their small claws.

We cannot hang.
We have no claws.

We must stay on the great plain.

II

The sun is a large body of fire
journeying
over the plain.

The stars are small suns,
homes of ghosts
and dead spirits.

Wakoñda lives on the great plain.
Wakoñda lives on the sun.
Wakoñda lives in the stars.

Wakoñda is the Great Power.
Wakoñda is the Great Mystery.
Wakoñda is the Great Eye.
Wakoñda is everywhere.

III

Wakoñda says,
When trouble comes
I put a cloud
across the moon.
I put a hand
to cover the moon.
I put something
I cannot name
to shadow the moon.

I hide the moon
to shield you
from trouble.

IV

Moon is a large Man,
holding a kettle in each hand,
giving us light.

Moon has many names:
Sore eye moon,
Frog moon,
Buffalo calf moon,
Hot moon.

Moon has other names:
Lengthening of days moon,
Lengthening of days moon's brother,
Snow-melting moon,
Moon when the buffaloes become fat.

Moon has many seasons:
Yellow-leaf moon,
Leaf-falling moon,
First snow moon,
Middle moon.

Moon counts time:
Moon and a full,
Four moons and an eaten one,
Six moons and an increasing one.

Moon is a large Man,
holding a kettle in each hand
to give us light.

V

We-as-poo-gah,
the moles,
the moon-nibblers,
live on the prairies.

Their noses are burned.
They have no teeth.
They burrow in the ground
but find nothing to eat.

Once, long ago,
They nibbled the moon
with their sharp teeth.
They ate it up.

They have been punished.

Wakoñda was angry.
He cast them down
to the prairies.
Wakoñda made a new moon.

Now, other we-as-poo-gah
with sharp teeth
and pointed noses
eat up the moon.

They will lose their teeth.
Their noses will be burned off.
Wakoñda will cast them down
and make another moon.

They will be punished.

SNAILS

Clinging to our stucco wall,
holding tight,
they never fall.

Resting on a zinnia stem,
they nibble leaves.
I look at them,

tracing their path
of sticky slime,
wondering where I would climb

if I could ooze a shining trail,
if I could travel
like a snail.

SONG OF THE OSAGE WOMAN

Footprints I make!
    Smoke arises from burning of the old stalks.
Footprints I make!
    The soil lies mellowed.
Footprints I make!
    The little hills stand in rows.
Footprints I make!
    Lo, the little hills have turned gray.
Footprints I make!
    Lo, the hills are in the light of day.
Footprints I make!
    Lo, I come to the sacred act.
Footprints I make!
    Give me one grain, two, three, four.
Footprints I make!
    Give me five, six, the final number seven.
Footprints I make!
    Lo, the tender stalk breaks the soil.
Footprints I make!
    Lo, the stalk stands amidst the day.
Footprints I make!
    Lo, the blades spread in the winds.
Footprints I make!
    Lo, the stalk stands firm and upright.
Footprints I make!
    Lo, the blades sway in the winds.
Footprints I make!
    Lo, the stalk stands jointed.

Footprints I make!
  Lo, the plant has blossomed.
Footprints I make!
  Lo, the blades sigh in the wind.
Footprints I make!
  Lo, the ears branch from the stalk.
Footprints I make!
  Lo, I pluck the ears.
Footprints I make!
  Lo, there is joy in my house.
Footprints I make!
  Lo, the day of fulfillment.
                    (Adapted from an Osage Indian song)

This song is sung in honor of the soil as it is prepared
for the sacred act of planting corn in the seven blessed
hills. It honors the stages of growth, the bearing of
fruit, and the harvest that is the renewal of duty and joy.

SPRINKER ICE ARENA

(FOR HEIDI GALLASCH)

There are brackets
    and rockets
    and edge jumps
    and toe

    but I start with waltz jumps
    (the kind that I know).

I take off my guards.
I lace up my skates.
My scribe makes the circles.
I do figure eights

    and practice my edge jumps
    and toe jumps, and think

    of a time I'll be skating
    a crystal-white rink
    doing axels and triples
    and landing them right

    (I'm wearing a blue dress
    with beads shiny bright)

    and the day comes at last
    when my dream will unfold:
    I am there! the Olympics
    and going for Gold!

STARS

I will imagine
  in my hand
  ten thousand shining grains of sand.

Ten thousand grains
  my fingers hold.
  Imagine, if I could enfold

All of the sand
  on every shore
  of planet Earth, there are still more

Stars out in space
  than grains of sand
  drifting the shores of beach-swept land.

Two hundred billion
  stars to see
  twinkling in our galaxy;

Young stars, blue stars
  glimmer and pass,
  born out of clouds of dust and gas.

Hot, yellow dwarf stars
  burn, and one
  fiery star we call our sun.

Red, black, white stars
  birthed long ago
  live in a place I'll never know.

Two hundred billion
  grains of light
  lost in the blackened shores of night.

TURTLE

We found him down at Turtle Creek,
Reached in the water and pulled him out,
His back all sticky with muck and slime.
We didn't take him home that time
But Saturday he was still about
So we brought him home. It's been a week.

He has a bowl of his very own
With a rock to climb on, a giant one.
The minute we scraped the slime off him
He played in the water and tried to swim.
But mostly he sits on the rock to sun
And he likes it here, where he's not alone.

VALENTINE HEARTS

Hi kid, says lavender.
Hug me, says blue.
Cutey, says yellow.
Pink says, How-R-U?

Love me, says purple.
So fine, says white.
Kiss me, says lemon.
Red says, All right.

THE VET

He cries all the way when we go to the vet.
He must remember he's been there before.

He howls and sings when we sit and wait
And trembles and shakes on the waiting-room floor.

He likes Dr. Keagy, who's gentle with him.
Dr. Winters is kind. He likes him too.

But it's hard to explain to a frightened dog
That whatever he's given, whatever they do,

Like a vaccination or pill or shot,
Isn't to make him howl or cry.

He smiles and pants when the doctors are through
And strains at the leash. And so do I.

WORKING WITH MOTHER

Some of the time
I get on the bus
with mother
(just the two of us)

and we go to the place
where she works all day.

We take some games
so I can play,

and some of the time
I help a lot
with work that mother

        just forgot
        (or couldn't finish —
        or did all wrong —)

        It's good
        she needs me
        to come along.

ENVOI: WASHINGTON SQUARE PARK

(FOR MARGARET K. McELDERRY)

Wind in the park
and the children swing
in the world of the green

in the wind on the leaves
and the children shout
in the wind in the park

and the joggers sprint
and the small birds sing
in the world of the green

and the dogs run free
and birds fly about
in the wind in the park

and the children go
and the light fades out
in the wind in the park
in the world of the green

16290